CALCULATED

Chapter 1

I must admit, I thoroughly enjoy watching you lose your mind. Questioning your sanity, trying to catch me in a lie. You think I'm like you. But the truth is, I'm much more calculated. That's one of the first adjectives I used to describe myself when we met. Calculated. I watch as you pace back and forth, listen in on my conversations from outside of the door, etc. As if I'm really that stupid. No, that's you. I can see the wheels turning in your head as you drive yourself crazy. It's pretty amusing, like watching a child waiting for Santa the night before Christmas.

Once I learned how to take my power back, the game changed. Honestly, I'm beginning to grow a little bored. I lacked the excitement I desperately craved in my life.

My phone alarm for me to leave the house startled me as I was lost in my thoughts. Mark handed me my purse. His tired eyes met mine. It was like he was trying to peer into my soul for the answers he snooped for. Maybe it was my guilty conscious convincing me of his motives. Either way, his gaze instantly annoyed me. I snatched my purse from his hands, grabbed my coffee, and rushed out the door. No words were needed, nor were they exchanged. We had been through enough. I was emotionally drained.

My phone beeped as I slammed my car door. It was work. They knew not to bother me before I got to the office. Running your own company was already tiring enough. When I'm not in the office, I'm off the clock. Everyone knew this. I assumed it must be the new intern texting me this early in the morning. I didn't bother to even look at the text message. Something else was on my mind.

My stomach quivered as flashbacks blazed through my head. Mmmm… I moaned beneath my breath. Remembering him deep inside me with my legs in the air, my thoughts quickly switched to his head between my thighs. Best head I've ever had, honestly. I couldn't help myself. I called him.

"Good morning," he yawned. I could tell he was stretching. The sound of his voice made me smile. We had undeniable chemistry. The kind of chemistry that you could feel just by being in the same room.

"Hey baby, I was just thinking about you. I wanted to hear your voice." I felt like a giddy schoolgirl all over again. I loved the feeling that he gave me.

"You miss me or something?" He chuckled beneath his breath. I didn't miss him, per se. I just loved the way he made me feel. I'm not like everyone else. Feelings confuse me. Some feelings I felt more intensely than others, while other feelings I could barely feel at all.

"Yea… something like that. You busy today?" The quivering feeling moved from my stomach down to my toes. My toes curled. It had been two weeks since we had seen each other, and I was long overdue for our special time.

"I've been busy, but I think I can make something shake." I rolled my eyes knowing he was full of shit. He always responded so surely even though we both knew he always struggled to make time for me due to his schedule. I think it was a way to keep me hooked, to tease me. He always made me want to come back for more, even though I knew I would have to wait for him to make time.

"Whatever, that's what you always say. I'm not going to ask again" I regretted calling him. I had been asking to see him for the past week. At this point, I felt like I was begging. Our relationship is complicated, to say the least. Our clashing schedules added to the mix and didn't help our situation.

"You don't have to ask again, I promise." The sound of his voice sucked me back in. I was a sucker for him, and I hated it. He got me every time. Whatever he wanted, whenever he wanted, he could have me.

"Ok baby, let me go. I just got to the office." I hung up the phone after he said his goodbyes and all that came with it. I'm not a fan of goodbyes. I say what I need to say and leave or hang up.

I parked my car and fixed my lipstick before heading inside. As I said before, we were nothing short of complicated. I was married, and he had a… situation. He and his girlfriend had been on and off for a while. I never knew when they were together and when they weren't, and I didn't care. To me, it seemed like he always acted like they were together. She always seemed to fall right back into place, playing her role as the perfect girlfriend.

He and I had an unspoken understanding that we would never be a thing, especially since we both had "situations". What is understood doesn't need to be discussed or explained. We both knew what it was. He also knew I was never going to leave my husband. He didn't understand it, but he knew it. It wasn't for him to understand. I keep my relationships separate. Two completely different worlds. That's how I preferred it to be.

I headed inside and strutted directly to my office. My assistant headed in right behind me. I sat down, throwing my bag down by my side.

"Anna, would you please explain to me why I got a text message from the office this morning before I got to work." I raised my eyebrows as I sipped from my coffee cup.

"Yes, we had a patient off his meds threatening everyone in front of the building before you got here." Anna explained. I tilted my head to the side.

I am in the mental health business. I have been running my own practice for five years. It was a very successful mental health and self-care facility. This was nothing new or outrageous, given the field that we are in.

"This couldn't have been handled without me?" I raised an eyebrow; my head still cocked to the side.

"Yes, ma'am. I believe it was the new secretary. She panicked and didn't know what to do." Anna nervously pushed her glasses up on her face.

"Who's the psychiatrist assigned to said patient?" I could feel myself getting annoyed once again. My period must be coming, or I'm overdue for my dick appointment.

"Dr. Graham. He was here when this happened and was able to get the patient calmed down and diffuse the situation. The patient was no longer on insurance and had an-" I put my hand up, cutting her off.

"That's enough. I get the point. Make sure this doesn't happen again. Hold a meeting or whatever you need to do to make sure nobody is contacting me before I reach the office. Thanks." I shewed her away, ready to get to my work. I didn't take clients anymore. I was the oil to make sure everything ran smoothly.

Inside my clinic, we had different departments set up. The therapist and psychiatrist section works closely together for those struggling with their mental health. Then there's the life coaches' side that specialized in different niches. Lastly, we have a state-of-the-art spa that's dedicated to self-care. I had created a whole experience. I'm more than proud of what I managed to build. From the ground up, with my husband by my side.

I would be lying if I said all of our years together were all great years. Every marriage or relationship, for that matter, had its ups and downs. My marriage was no exception. I would describe it as a never-ending rollercoaster, full of ups and downs. That's part of the reason why I started talking to Daniel on the side. It was an escape.

I decided to do my rounds and walk around my facility, ensuring everything was running smoothly, as I did every morning. I loved the sound of my heels clicking against the laminate floors. It made me feel important, like I had made it. It was the sound of success. I stopped to talk to some of the employees.

I made my way to the front desk of the mental health section of the clinic. I gave a sinister glare to the new secretary, purposely not speaking to her. Andrea, I believe, is her name. Her name is as annoying as she is. I do, however, see some of my younger self in her. Nervous, scared to make a mistake, but still aiming for perfection. I could cut her some slack, but I believe I could teach her a thing or two. Andrea purposely avoided eye contact with me. Someone must have warned her I was coming. She must've gotten chewed out by her supervisor for texting me this morning.

"Isla, how are things this morning?" I asked the other secretary who had been with the facility since the beginning. She must have forgotten a few important lessons to teach Andrea. The most important being, do not disturb me.

"Everything is running smoothly, ma'am." Isla smiled, looking up at me. I glanced around the room. It was fairly busy. I knew things weren't running as smoothly as Isla was letting on. Especially with the episode they had this morning. I appreciated her for keeping it all together. Isla was one of my hardest workers.

"That's what I like to hear." I said, glaring at Andrea.

"And Dr. Graham?" I questioned just for the hell of it, knowing she knew better than to give me all the details. I wanted Mia to see how Isla handled a situation like this.

"Dr. Graham is fine. Everything is under control ma'am, I promise." Isla answered, peering at Andrea like my husband had done to me this morning. Their gazes were like they were trying to peer through the depths of your soul. I tapped my fingers on the desk, giving Isla a head nod.

Just then, my work phone went off. It was Anna telling me someone was waiting for me in my office. I knew I didn't have any appointments, so I wasn't sure who it was. I marched to my office, beginning to feel annoyed yet again. Today was not starting on a good note. I stormed into my office, passing Anna's desk as she pointed in the direction of my office.

I knew who it was by the back of their head. I sat in my chair folding my hands together. Daniel stood up out of his chair and walked toward me.

"I told you that you wouldn't have to ask again." Daniel put one hand around my neck, bending down to kiss me. I was upset that he showed up at my office with no notice. My job was a completely different world. I didn't need my separate realities colliding.

I had a pattern of compartmentalizing everything in my life. My home life was one world, my side piece was another, and my job was a different world. Everything had its place. My worlds didn't mix, preferably. I showed Daniel where I worked once, but him showing up here was crossing the line, merging worlds. I didn't like that. It was unacceptable.

I could feel that feeling creeping up in my stomach again. Our soft lips met as he kissed me. His oversized hands gently squeezed my neck. I loved it.

"You can't be showing up here, Daniel." I pulled away. I watched as a sneaky grin crept onto his face. The chemistry in the room was thick.

"Why not?" Daniel's hands slid up my thigh. We peered into each other's eyes. I wanted to tell him to stop, not because I wanted him to but because I should.

"You couldn't make time for me outside the office?" I snapped, bringing myself back to reality. He was sneaking behind his girlfriend's back. I wish he didn't have to; then he would be able to make more time for me. I know it's selfish. I didn't care. I didn't care about his girlfriend or their relationship. Daniel rolled his eyes, making his way back around my desk. He settled back into his seat.

"Man, why you always gotta start." His southern accent rang in my ears. I found his accent quite amusing. This was another reason why I couldn't stay mad at him. Daniel's accent carried his humor. He didn't need to be funny.

"Why are you sneaking around? You guys aren't even together half the time, and you can't make time for me?" I just wanted him to leave. I wanted him out of my office. I also wanted answers as to why he couldn't make time for me. Daniel never gave me the answers, though.

"You got a whole man at home." Daniel was digressing as usual, which made me double down.

"Don't do that." I shook my head. We couldn't be around each other without some kind of disagreement or argument.

"Why you won't leave him? Why are y'all still together?" Daniel knew how and when to push the right buttons. I grinded my teeth. I'm not sure why he always asked these questions knowing we would never be together. That just wasn't our dynamic. Either way, he had no intent to be with me. His only purpose at the moment was to annoy me.

"Why do you ask so many questions? Why don't you leave your "sometime" woman for good?" The words flew right out of my mouth. Daniel chuckled; he never took me seriously, no matter how upset I was.

Daniel could tell I was growing irritated, but it never phased him. That's another thing I liked about him. He knew how to handle me and was slow to anger. I can't recall a time he's gotten upset with me. That was my role.

I was the one always getting upset. I squinted to study him. He always liked to peer into my other worlds. That wasn't his place. He knew his place, however sometimes he liked to test the boundaries.

"I'm just sayin'." he tried defending himself.

"I'm just saying find a day to get away. It can't be that difficult." I was about to kick him out. I did not feel like arguing today, but it was inevitable every time we were together. I always wondered why that was. Maybe it was because we both wanted each other to give more than we could.

"Alright, I'll get us a hotel. What's the best day for you?" Daniel stood up, walking toward me again. I could tell he was studying my face to see how much further he could push. Before I could answer, he bent down to kiss me again. This time his hands found their way up my skirt. I bit his lip, bracing myself for what he would do next. He moved my panties to the side and knew exactly where to place his fingers. I closed my eyes, knowing I was going to kick him out soon. I pushed his arm away and made eye contact. Daniel smirked and bit his lip. I knew he was about to push the boundaries a little further to see how far he could go. The truth is, I didn't know the extent of the boundaries either. When would I say stop? How could I bring myself to stop him? I wished someone would knock on the door or call my phone, but they knew better.

Daniel got on his knees and pulled me closer to him. He pushed my skirt up and moved my panties to the side. Daniel, Daniel. I repeated his name in my head but couldn't bring myself to form actual words. Once he put his mouth on me, all bets were off. Any logical thought I had left my head entirely. I pushed his head closer to me so I could be devoured. My eyes rolled to the back of my head. I wanted to tell him to stop, but I couldn't. I liked it too much. The lines I had drawn were becoming blurred. I could see my worlds merging. Unacceptable. I plopped my feet on my desk while he was still between my legs. I was enjoying this too much.

"Stop!" Suddenly, I pushed him away trying to catch my breath from all the moans I had held in. I removed my feet from the desk; we stood up simultaneously. I pulled my skirt down. I could tell he was satisfied with himself and so was I, to a certain extent.

"Tomorrow? I'll be there." I said, strutting towards the door to show him out. He slowly walked out, grinning from ear to ear. Oh, how I wanted him to stay, but I had to maintain some sort of control. Daniel had to know his place.

All I could think about for the rest of the day was our encounter. I tried my best to push it out of my mind. I tried focusing on what I would have for dinner. Spaghetti… no. Baked chicken… no, too basic. I was feeling feisty today. I wanted something… different. Maybe some scallops and paella. Yes, I think that's what I'll make for dinner.

After getting home, I turned on my slow jams, poured myself some red wine, and began to make dinner. I made love to my food. I mean, I really took my time putting my all into this meal. Daniel had left me on a high. I set the table and sat down for a quiet dinner with my husband.

"So, how was work?" I asked, trying to start a conversation. Mark partnered with one of his friends to start their own law firm. I was more than proud of them. We both immersed ourselves in our work to be successful. I think that's when our marriage became a failure. When we found our individual success, neither of us focused on our marriage anymore. Both of us was all about self.

"Work was fine. Busy, to say the least. I had a client that wanted me to go pro bono. I don't know who referred him to me-"

"Pro bono?" I cut him off, pretending to care. I just wanted to stay engaged in the conversation somehow. I didn't care about the law or lawyer mumbo jumbo. It all bores me, honestly.

"Right. I don't even know how he got through to me. I guess I'll have to talk to my secretary about that. Letting clients through that aren't worth my time." Aaah, the infamous secretary. I'm sure he's slept with his secretary many times in the past. I'd call it an ongoing affair. I had caught him many times, but I never called him out for it. It wasn't worth my time. Plus, I never wanted him to wonder what I was doing. I let him cheat in peace so that I could do the same. Mark wasn't as calculated as me. He was quite sloppy, in fact. Sloppy and nosy. Maybe his secretary wasn't doing her job keeping him happy. That's why he was trying to be all in my business, spying, and prying. Mark took a sip of his wine.

"You did want to become a lawyer to help people, honey. Have you lost sight of your purpose? That was the reason you started, right?" I stuffed piece of a scallop in my mouth, reminding him but also challenging him.

"Of course not, Daphne, I…" Mark stopped midsentence, noticing his mistake.

"Daphne… Is that her name?" I snickered. This was the perfect excuse to go soak in my bath instead of entertaining a conversation I didn't care to have. Mark dropped his head. He realized he had busted himself out.

"Cynthia, no. I just slipped up." Mark sighed, knowing he didn't make it any better.

"Oh, I know." I said, giving him a hard time. I wanted him to know that I knew. Men were nothing less than sloppy. As I mentioned before, I am much more calculated than he is. I got up from the table, taking my wine with me. I made my way to my tub. I had been waiting for this bath all day long, especially after my visit with Daniel.

The bath filled. I could feel the hot steam coming up from the water. Extra hot, just how I liked it. I turned on my music, lit my candles, turned the lights off, and slowly slipped into the tub. I let out a sigh of relief and laid my head back.

I imagined Daniel between my legs. He was all I could think about. I wish this giddy schoolgirl feeling would escape me. I mean, how old am I? I rubbed my head and took a sip of my wine. I wonder if he thinks about me as much as I think about him. I doubt it. I don't think he cares that much. I'm just something to do in his spare time, and I'm ok with that. I started singing lowly with the music. Suddenly the door swung open. I closed my eyes. I knew Mark had been listening at the door again. I could see his shadow at the threshold.

"Cynthia. I know there's nothing I can say to you to make you believe me, but… I'm not cheating on you. That was in the past. I made you a promise." Mark stood there, waiting for my reaction. I refused to give him one. I laid still, and silent with my eyes shut, hoping he would find his way out of my space. He did not.

"Who is Daphne?" I questioned, giving him the attention he desperately craved. I genuinely could not care any less. But he wanted me to entertain his foolishness, so I played along. Mark sat on the edge of the tub.

"Daphne is one of my clients." Mark was studying my eyes again, looking for a sign of whether he should continue with his explanation. Mark was trying to figure out whether he should tell the truth or tell a lie.

"Even better. Let me guess. She's going through a divorce?" I scoffed. Mark let his head hang low. The feeling of righteousness overcame me because that was his way of confirming what I said. I took a sip of my wine before throwing it in his face and placing the empty glass on the edge of the tub. I felt compelled to chuck it at the wall, but I didn't feel like cleaning up the mess or getting a sliver of glass stuck in my foot.

"Get out. You disgust me, honestly." I watched as he walked out the door. The only person I wanted was Daniel. Whenever something went wrong in my relationship, Daniel was all I could think about. I desperately yearned for his presence. In these moments; moments where I felt I had failed in my marriage, Daniel was who I wanted to be around. I grabbed my phone and texted him. It was late so I didn't know if he would reply. Even if it was a one-word reply I would be satisfied, I just needed to talk to him.

What time tomorroww?

I didn't know if he was at his (not)girlfriend's house or his own. Sometimes he spent the night at her place. I didn't ask many questions about his situation. I didn't care to know, honestly. My only concern was about what we had going on. Their relationship was something I had also compartmentalized.

He texted back with the eggplant emoji. I rolled my eyes holding back a smile as I got out of the bath. I used to analyze my marriage. About how we got here. Where had the passion gone? It used to bother me, but when I began focusing solely on myself, my failing marriage didn't bother me so much anymore.

The older I got, the more I realized everyone was for themselves. Everyone around me was self-absorbed. People didn't care about others' feelings or the well-being of others. Everyone did what they wanted when they wanted. They did what was best for them. With no regard for how their actions and decisions affected those around them or those who cared about them. If I was worried about everyone else and they were also worried about themselves, then who was worried about me? Who cared about me? If even my husband showed he didn't give a damn, how could I trust anyone else to care about me? I knew I couldn't trust anyone but myself. The day that I realized that I never trusted another soul again. It was the most significant decision I had made for myself.

Chapter 2

I woke up feeling refreshed. I credited it to Mark sleeping on the couch. I had the whole bed to myself. When Mark was in bed, I was usually pushed to the edge while he slept peacefully in the middle. It became normal for me to wake up with a stiff neck and a sore back. However, this morning I woke up feeling brand new, but I still needed a little extra rejuvenation. I was looking forward to noon.

I took extra time getting ready this morning. I put an extra layer of mascara on. I slowly slid my lipstick across my lips. Red. Red is sexy. I usually didn't go for this color unless I was in the mood. I read this study once that claimed men are more attracted to women when they wear red. It's not something that men usually notice. It was more of a subconscious attraction. But I knew, and I was intentional when I wore it. Many women go with lingerie colors like pink or black. Pink is for little girls. Black is for professional settings like work meetings or, worse, funerals. But red, red is sexy. Always go with the red.

Mark's reflection appeared in the mirror, interrupting my thoughts, which he had been doing a lot lately. I pretended he wasn't there. Although, I did get a thrill out of him watching me. His eyes moved up and down my body. He appeared absent-minded per usual. It was as if he couldn't find the words to say.

"Cynthia… I want better for us." He had the eyes of a sad puppy dog. I cleaned up the lipstick from around my mouth, making sure my lipstick was nice and neat. Mark knew what it meant when I wore red. Perhaps he thought I was doing it out of spite for him "slipping up" last night. If he only knew.

"Goodbye, Mark." I grabbed my clutch and headed to work.

When I got there, everything was running smoothly as usual.

"Anna." I greeted her, walking past her desk. Anna followed me into my office, standing at attention as if she was waiting for her next set of orders. Which, she kind of was.

"I am only going to be here for a while. I'm leaving around eleven thirty. I'll be out of the office for the rest of the day. Is there anything you or anyone else needs from me?" I waited patiently as she looked over her notes. I was not as irritated today; I was in a great mood.

"Nope. I believe we've got everything under control." Anna said as she finished glossing over her notes. I waved my hand in the air excusing her. I didn't like to waste time, even if I had nothing to do.

I looked through some emails and responded to a few of them. Mark was texting me like crazy. It was harassment at this point. I didn't open a single one of his messages. I didn't care to. I wasn't in love with him anymore, so nothing he did bothered me. It had been a while since I had been in love. I missed the feeling. Being in love is one of the best feelings in the world. Falling out of love kind of happens fast, all at once, and without warning. Things begin to get stale and you start irritating one another. Falling out of love is inevitable, in my opinion. Love doesn't last, so you might as well find a good teammate to go through life with. That was my philosophy. It wasn't until recently that I began to question if Mark was a good life partner, a good teammate.

Being alone isn't so bad, either. I prefer it, actually. You can do what you want when you want, with little to no consequences. You don't have to explain yourself to anyone because you owe them no explanation. You can be...selfish, like everyone else.

At exactly 11:30 a.m. I grabbed my clutch and rushed to the hotel. Daniel had texted me the room number while I was lost in my emails at work. I couldn't wait to get there. When I arrived, the door was cracked open. He had the old, slow jam love songs playing. I closed the door behind me. Daniel had always gotten suites. He didn't like regular hotel rooms. He needed to feel like he was in a home or something; it made him more comfortable. I didn't mind either way. I was there to get a job done, not to play house. The suite had a living room, bedroom, and kitchen area. It was nice and the view was amazing. He was coming out of the bathroom that was in the back of the suite. He had his shirt off. I couldn't help but stare. He was built but not like a bodybuilder. You could tell he worked out regularly. He had a four-pack and a V. Oh, how I loved his V.

"Come on." Daniel nodded towards the bedroom. I loved that he could take charge and demand me around. He was the only one that could do that. I was in control of everything else in my life. It felt great to let someone else take the lead for a change. I was getting all hot and bothered. I could feel my stomach filling up with butterflies. I entered the bedroom. Daniel followed behind me. He put his arms around my waist and kissed gently on my neck. Daniel was rough around the edges but knew when to be soft. He nudged me towards the bed. Daniel bent me over onto the bed. He quickly took off his sweatpants while I pulled up my dress. I couldn't wait. I would take the dress off later. He shoved himself inside of me. I let out a loud moan. In and out. It was like we were performing an intricate dance. I tightly gripped the duvet. Deep. Too deep. I pushed against him to create distance between us.

Daniel pulled out and turned me over, changing positions. He put both of my legs on his shoulders. He was still standing on the side of the bed while I was lying on it. I knew I would be in all kinds of positions and folded up like a pretzel at some point. Now he was even deeper. I cried out even louder. I think he liked when I was loud. I could see flames in his eyes with every moan I let out. Again, I pushed him away from me. He grabbed my wrist and pinned it above my head. Yes. Yes. This is what I needed. This is what I was waiting for. He didn't let up. He didn't stop. I knew we were going to be going for a while. We missed each other. We could always tell each other how much we missed the other person.

"I love you!" A tear escaped from the side of my eye as I exhaled. Fuck. The notorious *I love you.* Forbidden. These were forbidden words to us. It was an unspoken understanding we had. There was no love. Lust. Just lust. The truth was I didn't love him. I wasn't in love with him. I had love *for* him. Maybe I was too into my thoughts. Perhaps the sex was that good. I loved the sex, not him. I hoped he didn't hear me and we could sweep this under the rug. After another hour, we finished.

"So, you love me huh?" Daniel put his shirt back on, grinning like a Cheshire cat. Embarrassed, I rushed to put my clothes on. I was tossing the sheets around trying to find my panties. They were tangled and intertwined between the different layers of the sheets. Daniel started to chuckle after he realized I was ignoring him. His laugh was like nails on a chalkboard. I cringed.

"I lust after you. I don't love you; I love the sex." Control. I had to stay in control. I couldn't stroke his ego. I had stroked enough. I couldn't let him feel like he was "the man". Men loved that shit, they ran with it. Annoying. I met his gaze. Our eye contact was intense and passionate. Blurting out the truth made me want to jump his bones again, or maybe it was the way he looked at me.

"Yea? Well, I lust you too." He started putting his shoes on. I just wanted to grab him. I did not want this moment to end. I mean, did he actually lust for me? Of course he did. We wouldn't be here if he didn't. We already established there's no love there. I had love for the man, a passion for him, but I wasn't in love. I'd like to say he was disposable, but he wasn't. Even if we didn't talk for a year or two, something always pulled us back together. One of us always missed or lusted after the other. He stood up after putting on his shoes, walked over to me, and gave me a peck before trying to head out. After he pulled from me, I yanked him back in by his arm. I kissed him passionately. Neither of us wanted this to end. Sappy. I wasn't the sentimental type. We weren't sappy with each other. Sometimes we didn't even kiss. The lines were becoming blurred.

Confusion was starting to set in. I held my head down biting my lips. It was time to go. We finally said our goodbyes and returned to our separate, intertwined lives. Intertwined like my panties were in the sheets. There was no escaping from each other. Over the years, I waited for him to cut me off, ignore me, hurt my feelings, something that would prevent us from messing with each other. But he never did. That's why it continued so long. Twin flames? Soul ties? Perhaps, I didn't know much about that kind of stuff, but one couldn't help but question it. What was this? I didn't know, but back to my regular boring life I went.

When I got home Mark had a candlelit dinner on the table. Great. Now I had to pretend like I cared. I had to pretend that I was heartbroken that my husband had been cheating on me. The truth is, I knew he had been doing this for years. It's why I withdrew from him. My feelings for him were nonexistent. I took a deep breath trying to get into character. Play my role. I sat my bag down and sat in the chair opposite him. I picked up the glass of wine. A thought quickly flashed in my mind. What if he was trying to kill me? I covertly inspected the glass and put it right back down without taking a sip. I didn't say a word.

"Baby, I love you. I want this to work. What I'm going to say is difficult, to say the least. I want to be honest with you. In the past, I was dishonest, disloyal, and sloppy. But I want to start fresh. I want to start over. I have been loyal; I haven't done anything. I told you the truth when I said Daphne is a client and I haven't done anything with her." Mark took several deep breaths in between his sentences. I had all intention to play the role and pretend to care tonight but I didn't have the energy. Being around Mark completely drained me. I was over it. Just take me out now. I took a sip of the wine— the wine he might have poisoned. I felt like having some fun tonight. Tonight, I was going to test the waters.

"Mark, how would you feel if I were to do the same thing?" I rested a piece of steak on my lips, holding it up with a fork. I watched as the discomfort settled over him. I enjoyed watching him squirm in his seat.

"It goes without saying that I wouldn't like that. That's not something I would want, obviously. I know what I did was wrong." Mark nervously gulped his wine. I stuck my tongue out of the side of my mouth, cocked my head back, and closed my eyes. I was "playing dead". I had no genuine interest in this conversation, I only wanted to have fun. Lately, I had been acting on impulse. I wasn't sure why, but I liked it. It was fun. Maybe it was the new me. I busted out in laughter. Mark looked more confused than ever. He looked at me like I was going crazy. Maybe I was. Mark looked scared. If I were in his position, I would be scared too. I couldn't stop laughing. Seeing the expression on his face induced more laughter. I couldn't get myself under control. Control. It's something I thrived on. I had to have control. I stopped my laughter abruptly and started to analyze myself. Sudden irritability, loss of control over my thoughts, impulse control issues. These were symptoms of Intermittent Explosive Disorder (IED). It came unexpectedly and without warning. Suddenly, shit wasn't so funny anymore. But… I liked this new me. Maybe acting on impulse was good for me, losing control was good for me. I frowned down at the table as these thoughts quickly raced through my mind. I looked up at Mark. He was overcome with fear. I liked that; he deserved it. I got up from the table and went to bed, leaving him there alone. I'm sure he felt dazed and confused. He probably had a whole speech prepared and I ruined it just like he had ruined our marriage. Remorse. I didn't know the feeling of remorse. My every move was deliberate. I planned my whole life out. Before I made a decision, I thought about the outcome of my actions. I carefully moved through the world. I made no excuses. There was nothing for me to be remorseful about, ever. And I wasn't going to start now.

When I woke up the following morning, I took a long hot shower. I exfoliated, put on my mud mask, and let the scolding hot water run down my body. I took my time putting on my makeup in the mirror. I thought maybe Mark might come and bother me, but he didn't. I went downstairs to look for him, but he had already left the house. He probably didn't have the energy to put into another awkward conversation. Neither did I. I wanted to keep my peace protected.

When I got to work, I did my rounds and sent Daniel a text after settling at my desk. I scrolled through emails and checked only the ones that seemed important. I was bored. Everything I had once been passionate about was boring. I did not want to be at work right now. I wanted to be outside enjoying the fresh, crisp air. I loved the cold foggy California mornings. Taking that air into your lungs was indescribable, especially while jogging. There were so many other things I could be doing with my time besides sitting behind a desk in an office during my favorite weather.

I paged Anna, demanding she get me a hot upside-down caramel macchiato. Upside down. A lot like my life lately. I opened the window closest to my desk so that I could feel the cold air. Really feel it. I gazed out the window watching the cars down below. I imagined myself driving down the foggy highways. Something about the cold I have always loved. Maybe because it was like me. Cold.

A short while later, Anna walked in with my coffee. She always seemed nervous and in a rush. She was well put together but always had a few hairs sticking out perfectly imperfect.

"Thank you, Anna." Anna gave me a smile and a nod. I was bored so I decided to draw Anna in with a little conversation.

"How are you and your boyfriend?" I questioned. I didn't know if I was entirely interested or not. Anna did not seem like an interesting person, but you would be surprised at the lives people live. Humans are unpredictable. That's why I loved my job. I was always intrigued about people and the lives they led. What made them tick? Why do they do the things they do? Human behavior is fascinating.

"Oh, uhm. He died." Anna blurted out quickly.

"I'm sorry for your loss." I was never the one good at death or comforting others who were grieving. I took a sip of coffee not knowing what to do next.

"No, not literally. Just figuratively. I killed him off in my mind. He's dead to me." Anna gave a shy smile waiting for my reaction.

"Well, good for you Anna. I do ask though, that if you do kill someone, please refrain from telling me. I'm a terrible liar, and you will get caught." We laughed jokingly.

There was a knock on the door as a head peeked in.

"Hey!" It was my best friend, Nia. We had been friends since grade school. Blood couldn't make us closer sisters than we already were. Anna saw herself out, leaving us alone. Nia had bags in her hand. She set them on my desk and aggressively dug through them. I recognized the bag. It was food from Wing It, my favorite wing place. She pulled out a box and sat it in front of me and took out another box for herself. I was so glad she brought me lunch. I could really eat right about now. I shoved a fry in my mouth.

"Are you still talking to Daniel?" A grin ran across my face even though I tried to hide it. I raised my eyebrows and tilted my head down. Nia knew what that meant. I had a different facial expression for just about every thought I had. Nia recognized them all.

"Cynthia!" Nia exclaimed before asking me for all the juicy details. She loved the stories of my life even though she would scold me occasionally.

"Well, we saw each other yesterday." I answered knowing she would want more details but honestly there was nothing to say.

"Did you guys have sex?" She asked excitedly as if she was watching a drama-filled movie.

"Yes!" I laughed as the flashbacks zoomed through my head and my body.

"Cynthia, you have to stop girl." It seemed like this was going to be one of the times she was going to scold me.

"I know Nia! But I can't. I don't know why; I don't know what it is. Is this what they mean when they say soul tie… or what's the other one?" I said in a singsong voice. Almost like I was whining. I knew it wasn't right, but I wasn't planning on stopping any time soon.

"Twin flame?" Nia asked finishing my thought.

"Yes! Soul tie or twin flame. I don't know what the difference is but that's what he is to me. I can't let him go." Thoughts continued to run through my head. I knew this couldn't go on forever, but I couldn't see how it would end.

"The only twin flame, soul tie, twin tie, soul flame, whatever; you should have is with your husband. You should be talking about your husband, the love of your love, with the same passion you talk about." I could tell in Nia's eyes that she sympathized with Mark. She had been cheated on a couple of times. So much so that she stopped dating for a while, now she was starting to get her "groove back" again.

"Nia, whose side are you on?" I took a bite out of one of my wings and waited intently for her answer. Had she forgotten that he was a cheater? I didn't start this, but I was going to end it. Nia's eyes moved around the room. I could tell she was thinking.

"I…The right side. I'm on the right side." Nia hesitated to try to form her words. She stuck several fries in her mouth hoping she wouldn't have to speak again. She hated uncomfortable conversations, but she never missed a moment to let me know how she really felt.

"Did you forget he started this? He cheated first! That is the only reason why Daniel and I are a thing right now." The conversation was like a delicate game of chess. We each made our move (or statement) and carefully waited to hear the other's reply.

"Ok first, you and Daniel are not a thing. And why don't you just go to counseling with Mark so you guys can fix your marriage. Practice what you preach Cynthia!" Nia was letting me have it today. She was getting tired of my games as if I was doing this to her.

I rolled my eyes continuing to stuff my face. I didn't have a reply, but I had to carefully think of my next reply. It was my turn to make the next move.

"We both know that no amount of counseling will make Mark stop cheating, he's a serial cheater." Bingo! That was the perfect argument. As sad as it may be, it was the truth, and it was my excuse for continuing to do what I was doing. Everybody only cares about themselves. That's a hard truth you learn in the world. It doesn't matter what or how much you do for a person, they will always put themselves first, especially men.

"Then leave him, Cynthia! Simple as that. But this ain't it girl. You need to be happy." Nia judgingly shook her head slurping her drink.

"I can't leave, you don't understand, and I am happy." I was happy. I am happy. Other people may not understand the life I live and maybe they wouldn't be happy with it, but my life is perfect for me. I would say I'm happy in my truth, but I have a few skeletons in the closet.

"Why can't you leave?" Nia challenged.

"I just said Nia, that you wouldn't understand." I began to grow irritated. Mark was the only family I had ever known, flaws and all. I couldn't give up my only family.

"You're making excuses Cyn." Nia wouldn't let up. I knew there was no way I was winning this game of chess.

"And you should've just cheated back, Nia" The words flew out of my mouth before I could stop them.

"I left. Just remember that. I left." Nia glared at me in a condescending way.

After the exchange or the chess match rather, we exchanged a few laughs. Nia and I could always be honest with each other, and we never took it personally. Everybody needs a brutally honest friend. We finished our food and our chuckles between words, and she left. I knew Nia was right and I hated it. I didn't like anyone telling me what to do or telling me when I was wrong. But, when it came to Nia, it was different. She could always put me in my place. I mostly listened to what she had to say, but not this time. This time I took slight offense to her words. Offense; a feeling that rarely resonated with me.

I ended up getting home pretty late. I hated being there. Your home was supposed to be a safe haven, but this place was hell for me. I hated being here. The walls screamed depression. Deep, dark, dreadful. Suddenly, my phone beeped. It was a text message from Daniel. My eyes lit up as if I were a kid on Christmas morning. The text message was simple:

We need to talk

My heart sank to my stomach and the depressing walls started crumbling down around me. Those were the four deadly words. What could he want to talk about? I pushed the phone down in my back pocket and headed to take a shower.

The boiling water felt like silk sliding down my skin. I poured some lavender oils on the shower floor to help relax me. Suddenly the shower door flew open. Mark poked his head in.

"What the hell are you doing?" I shouted covering my breasts. My body was no longer his to gaze at whenever he wanted. I didn't look at him as my husband anymore.

"Baby, I love you." Mark tried looking into my eyes, but he couldn't hold his head up.

"Ugh, you stink! Are you drunk? Get out!" I threw words at him never giving him the chance to answer. I shoved him out of the shower and slammed the glass door shut. Great. I had a "come to Jesus moment" with Nia, I live in a depression box, I got a "we need to talk" text from Daniel, and now my shower was ruined. That was the kind of day it was. I got out and got dressed in my pajamas. There was a strong hate for Mark growing inside of me like a fetus. I fed it, I nurtured it, and it continued to grow. It was a part of me now. I couldn't see myself getting rid of it. I was attached. Attached to deep dark hatred and it was attached to me.

I didn't even care anymore about Mark's whereabouts or even who he was with. I just wanted him to leave me the hell alone. Watching him sulk around and be miserable was no longer entertaining to me. It all became annoying, bland, boring. I couldn't get Daniel out of my head. I couldn't stop imagining what life would be like with Daniel. What if I never met Mark? What if

Daniel and I decided to take each other seriously? Why couldn't we… Why couldn't we be? Our relationship seemed more intimate and mysterious. The unknown intrigued me. Maybe it was the mystery that attracted me. I felt like I was losing myself. Losing myself in him.

"Cynthia, can we talk?" Mark sat on the bed looking pitiful. Those four words were vexing coming from him. Just looking at him made my stomach churn. I just looked at him; pitiful and drunk. Disgusting. How did I get here? How did *we* get here?

"No drunkard, we can't. Goodnight."

"Cynthia…"

"You're lucky I said goodnight." I rolled over returning to my daydreams about Daniel.

When I got to the office, I called Daniel from my work phone. I tapped my pen against my desk nervously. What was he going to say? The phone rang continuously in my ear. I could feel my heart beating out of my chest. He didn't answer. My call went to voicemail. A text popped up on my screen:

Meet me at my place

I was excited to see him but still nervous. I hurriedly stuffed some paperwork into my bag and grabbed my coffee. I let Anna know I would be back soon.

After pulling up to his house, I and nearly fell out of my car trying to get out. Somehow, I had gotten tangled up in my seatbelt. I stopped for a second, very carefully untangling myself from the seatbelt like I was unraveling myself out of a web. Ironically, that felt like my life right now. After freeing myself, I took a couple of deep breaths and pulled myself together before heading in.

Daniel opened the door before I could reach it. He welcomed me in with a soft smile. He led me into the kitchen, and we both took our seats at the kitchen table. There was no food prepared. Just us and the table.

"Cynthia. There's no easy way to say this but… we can't do this anymore. This; whatever this is, is over." Daniel braced himself for my reaction.

There it was. The words I dreaded to hear. I knew it was coming but I wasn't ready to let go. I wasn't ready to let go of my fantasy that I desperately wanted to be my reality.

"Why?" I asked him sternly, shocked almost.

"I…" Daniel took a deep breath before he continued. "I'm going to try to make it work with Chantel." He explained.

"And… what does that have to do with me?" I was not going to accept this. Their relationship had nothing to do with me. It never had, why would it matter to me now?

"I want to be right. I want to do right this time. I have to change some things. I need to give my all to her. Why does it matter to you anyway? You have a man." Daniel tried putting the attention all on me. He was right, I did have a "man". I wasn't going to argue with him, He had every right to do what he wanted with his life. Even if I was unhappy about it.

"I don't understand why you need to bring him up. He has nothing to do with this, with us. Just like Chantel has nothing to do with us... Daniel don't do this" I tried one more time to change his mind. I refused to completely beg. Daniel looked down at the table taking a deep breath and shaking his head. I could tell he wasn't going to let up. He had made up his mind.

"Fine. Can we just…" I struggled to get the words out. "Make love one more time. As a final goodbye." Daniel looked up not looking so overwhelmed anymore.

"Yea, as a goodbye. Follow me to this room." Daniel stood up and led me upstairs to his bedroom. As I followed behind him, I observed the muscles in his shoulders and arms. That man had some strength, and I was about to feel it.

I sat on the bed and let him undress me. I took in the moment knowing it was going to be the last time. I knew I wouldn't ever feel this passion ever again. If I did, I knew it wouldn't be with Mark. My bra hit the floor. I laid back allowing him to take off my panties with his mouth. They hit the floor. I felt his mouth all over my body. He kissed my neck and worked his way down to my feet and then back up stopping in just the right spot. His tongue circled my clit repeatedly. He kissed each lip gently and individually. Kissing, sucking, caressing my pussy in his mouth. I could feel his tongue… everywhere. My toes curled and my eyes rolled to the back of my head. Daniel gave the best head I had ever had. When we first started sleeping together, he used to put in work. He would massage my whole body before even attempting to please me. I never had to ask; he always knew exactly what to do. Daniel slid his hand around my neck giving me a gentle choke. He moved from one set of lips to the ones on my face and slipped himself right inside of me. I let out a deafening moan. I was so wet. I wanted to stay focused on the moment. I couldn't help but think about how this was the last time. Our last time. Thoughts of our past flashed through my head. My mind flooded with our memories, good and bad. All the times I was mad at him and all the times he made me smile. He still gave me butterflies after all this time.

Daniel shoved my legs in the air thrusting himself deeper inside of me. My moans grew louder. I gripped the back of his neck pulling him closer to me. He pinned my arms to the bed. I tried kissing him but he hid his face in my neck. I didn't know if he regretted this moment but, this isn't what I expected. I couldn't enjoy it like I wanted to. Daniel shoved himself deeper and faster into me.

"You like that baby?" Daniel asked me. How the fuck was I supposed to answer that? He didn't deter from his regular sex talk but it caught me off guard. It was giving… mixed signals and I didn't like that. I stared deep into his soul without answering him. I wanted to slap him honestly. Daniel turned me over and I arched my back as if he wasn't already deep enough. I could hear his heavy breathing. He let out a small moan I could tell he tried to keep in. He was too deep, I tried reaching back and pushing him away from me. Daniel pinned my hand to the bed and slowed down but he was still deep. My arch dropped and my moans grew. This was exactly what I wanted but why couldn't it last? Daniel gave me all that he had and I took it. I took all of it. I didn't have it in me to return the favor. I was too hurt. He understood that.

When we finished, we quickly threw our clothes back on. I observed his face and his body language to get a sense of how he was feeling. I wondered if he felt like me or if he was happy to get rid of me.

"Look, I don't exactly know how you're feeling. I don't know if you truly want to stop" I gave one last attempt.

"I do." Daniel interrupted before I could finish my impromptu speech.

"So, what was that? Did you actually want to sleep with me or was that a pity fuck?" I began to grow angry. Not only was he cutting me off, but he didn't regret it. Daniel wanted this.

"Cynthia. I don't do anything that I don't want to do. I wanted to sleep with you one last time. I also want to do right by Chantel." Daniel tried reassuring me but I'm not sure that it worked.

"How long have you been feeling like you want to break things off? Are you tired of me or something, because Chantel has never had anything to do with us?" I wanted answers. I demanded them. Clearly, he didn't feel the same way about me that I felt about him.

"It's not you, it's my situation. Don't make this bigger than what it is." Daniel sat down on the bed. What an asshole. I was making this bigger than what it was? Not yet, but I would.

"You know what? You're right. This was going to come to an end somehow. Better now than later, right?" I was now trying to give myself reassurance. Daniel stood up and gave me a hug. I pulled back slightly standing on my tiptoes trying one more time to get a kiss out of him. He kissed me passionately. I still didn't know if this was a pity kiss. I tried hard to enjoy this last kiss. A goodbye kiss. Daniel walked me back downstairs to the front door and waved goodbye as I got in my car. This was far from over but he didn't know that yet.

Now I'm not the petty type. If you're thinking I was going to have a "woman to woman" conversation, you're wrong. No, I knew my place. That was an unspoken agreement in these types of situations, and I was going to play my role. I had no respect for anyone who did that. You knew what you signed up for. So, I would not be coming or going to anyone "as a woman". There would be no Shirley and Barbara conversations around here. I'm not petty at all. However, I could be much more calculated. Sinister even. I wasn't in love with the man, but I wasn't going to let too many more people play with my emotions without consequence.

I went back to the office and looked up Chantel on her social media pages. She was nothing like me. Not ambitious or well put together like me. She was sort of a hippy. "Spiritual" nature-loving woman was what you could describe her as. Chantel was beautiful, you couldn't take that away from her. She posted that she would be at some yoga event in the park this weekend. I rolled my eyes. Of course, she would be into yoga. I hated yoga. It's not real exercise. Although, I had done a Pilates class one time and found it quite difficult. I hated this girl and for no reason at all. Over a stupid asshole. I was never the type for "women empowerment" so hating a girl for no reason didn't bother me. Call me stupid or whatever, chances are, you've done it too. Chantel looked happy. She didn't appear to have any worry in the world. She was just a free hippie who didn't care what anyone thought of her. I could tell by her stained shirt, loose torn jeans, and her paint-splattered bandana on her head. I closed my browser. I could feel a slight bit of envy creep into the pit of my stomach. I didn't like to feel that way. After all, I am a woman on top of the world. Why would I be envious of some… some sloppy hippy? Happiness, maybe? Her happiness and her carefree lifestyle were what I was envious of. I couldn't lie to myself. It seemed like everything she wanted easily fell into her lap. Like she barely, if at all, had to work for anything. I knew exactly what I had to do.

Chapter 3

I found myself holding a small peach tea in my hand and a yoga mat underneath my arm in the middle of the park Saturday morning at 8 a.m. It was the earliest I had woken up on a Saturday morning in a while. I gazed at all the people unrolling their yoga mats and stretching to warm up for "Yoga in the park". I sipped my tea, peering across the park searching for the infamous Chantel.

"First time?" A voice snuck up behind me. Startled, I jumped. It was Chantel. She greeted me with a wide smile. Did she recognize me? Did she know who I was? I had to be meticulous and cautious in my conversation.

"How can you tell?" I smiled back.

"I come all the time and I never miss an opportunity to introduce myself to a new face. I'm Chantel." Her locs gently tickled the top of her shoulders. They were tied up in her bandana again but I could tell they were long. She held out her hand to introduce herself. My stomach began to feel queasy. I still couldn't tell if she knew who I was.

"Xen… it's short for Xenia. It's pronounced like Zen but it's spelled with an X." I shook her hand. I couldn't give her my real name but… Xen? Out of all names, this is what I came up with… at a yoga event. And the whole explanation? People usually include extra information when they lie so I hoped she couldn't tell that I was lying. I didn't think I would be this nervous.

"How fitting. I like that. Well, I guess you're in the right place Xen." There was something about her that mesmerized me. Her aura was invigorating. It was like she wanted to bring me into her world. Unbeknownst to her, I was already in it. Chantel began to unroll her mat right next to me. I followed her lead and did the same. We sat down together.

The yoga instructor took her place at the front and began to lead us. I forgot how hard yoga was. One stretch after the other, I could barely do them at all. Chantel gave me a couple of glimpses between poses. I wondered what she was thinking. She was probably trying to see how well I knew the poses. Perhaps she was trying to see if I looked familiar. After our eyes met, Chantel tried to pretend she wasn't looking at me. But I had already caught her. My breathing became labored. Sweat beads popped up on my forehead. One stretch I was staring at my toes, the next I was staring at my crotch.

Finally, we finished. I was so glad to be done. A cramp had formed in my thigh, and I was more than ready to go. I downed my tea, but it made me more thirsty. I carefully watched Chantel drink her water as I tried to catch my breath.

"Water?" Chantel offered me her gigantic, insulated water bottle. I could tell it was ice cold, it was tempting. Who offers a stranger their water? Surely, she knew who I was. Maybe there was poison inside. I was being paranoid. She had already drunk the water. I glared at the water bottle.

"Here you go. I don't believe in germs. Unless you have a cold sore which you clearly don't have. You need water. Here." Chantel practically shoved the water in my face.

"Thanks." I hesitantly took a drink of her water. She was right, I definitely needed it. It was ice cold and felt amazing going down. Who drinks a stranger's water? Technically, she wasn't a stranger, was she?

"Do you usually offer strangers your water?" I asked lightheartedly.

"Only when they bring tea to yoga." We gave each other a light chuckle. Chantel began rolling up her mat. Again, I followed her lead and did the same. She gathered her mat and her water bottle and walked away. I don't think she knew who I was.

"Hey!" I called out. Chantel stopped in her tracks and spun around with a big smile plastered on her face.

"Hey, do you want to… I don't know; grab coffee or something?" What am I doing? Inside I was telling myself "Stay calm. Don't freak out". Pretending like I wasn't a weirdo was harder than I expected. I wanted to get closer to her. I needed her to trust me. It's easy to control people when they trust you. I just hadn't decided what I would do with her yet. I couldn't be impulsive. This had to be one of my most calculated moves. Chantel paused for a moment. I waited anxiously for her answer. She looked up at the trees, her thoughts ran across her face.

"How about drinks instead?" Chantel smiled and bit her lip.

"Sure." I hesitated again.

"Cool. There's a jazz club downtown I like to go to. They play live music. Jazz, R&B, and reggae every now and then. It's called Blue Moon." I watched her speak. I didn't know if I was still envious. There was something about her. Something I couldn't put my finger on.

"Blue Moon." I repeated nodding.

"Cool. See you at seven."

"Seven." I repeated and nodded again. I was still unsure of what to say and wanted to be cautious of my words. Chantel turned and walked away.

I threw my tea in the trash and rushed home to shower.

After I got out of the shower, I went to my closet to decide what to wear for tonight at seven. Jazz club. I had to wear something… jazzy. I pulled out a burnt orange romper. It had a collar that hugged my neck, and the pants part was long and oversized. It fit loosely and looked like it could be a dress. It was perfect. Not too dressy but not too laxed either. I sat the romper on the bed and went to play around with my hair in the mirror. Should I wear it up or down? Maybe, half up and half down.

"You look nice." It was Mark. I just couldn't get rid of him. I could never have time to myself. I continued to play with different looks in the mirror. Mark walked over and kissed my shoulder. I instantly turned around and slapped him. He grabbed his face and hung his head down. Fuck! This damn explosive disorder. I had to gain control of myself.

"You know what Cynthia, I deserved that. I get it. But we have to figure out how to fix this."

"I am not responsible for fixing something you destroyed Mark. I tried! I have been trying for years. But you know what? I give up! I just want to focus on my own peace. So, if you would allow me to do that that would be great. Don't talk to me, don't touch me. Just don't." I started lotioning my body.

"I respect that." Mark walked out of our bedroom. I could hear him raise the garage to leave. Was I being too harsh? I couldn't care about that. I had to finally focus on myself and my needs. Needs. What were my needs exactly? I didn't really know, so how was I supposed to focus on them? I needed Daniel but I couldn't have him. So, I needed a plan. I lost Daniel, gained his girlfriend or whatever she was, and I was stuck with Mark. How was I going to make this right? My phone rang. Nia was calling. I didn't know if I should answer or not.

"Hey girl!" I answered.

"Hey! Do you want to go to Exotic tonight?" Exotic was my favorite nightclub. It was the only time I felt like I could really let loose. The only place where I could feel free. But I had already made plans with Chantel.

"I would love to go. You know I need it but, I don't feel good." I coughed. Nia couldn't know the truth. She knew I did some crazy things but I couldn't let her know just how crazy I could get.

"Oh no, Cyn. Well, I hope you feel better. Me and the girls will take a shot for you." I could hear the disappointment in her voice. She would be fine.

"Take a shot for meeee oh oh oh" I sang jokingly. We laughed.

"Ok lady. Take care of yourself and feel better. There's been something going around." We said our goodbyes and hung up the phone.

I did a few loads of laundry, did some charting, and checked work emails before getting ready to head to Blue Moon. I loved getting dressed up and doing my makeup. It made me feel like a woman. A feeling that is indescribable but also very amazing. I decided to put my hair in a high bun and give myself two bangs. It was the perfect look. I grabbed my clutch and headed out. I was glad I was able to get ready in peace.

I arrived exactly at seven not knowing if I should wait in the parking lot for Chantel or meet her inside. We had forgotten to exchange numbers, so there was no way of contacting her. I decided to just head inside. When I walked in, Chantel was on stage singing a slow song. It was as mesmerizing as she was. I found an empty table with two chairs and sat down. A cocktail waitress approached me to get my drink order.

"Cognac on the rocks." I told her as I watched Chantel on the stage. Her voice was angelic, very soothing. Of course, she's a singer. It sounded like an R&B/soul song. I loved it. She closed her eyes as she sang. You could tell she was really feeling her music. When she opened her eyes, our gaze connected. I took a sip of my drink. This girl was absolutely perfect! I mean, she couldn't be topped. She was extremely down-to-Earth, warm and inviting, and she could sing. What couldn't this girl do? I understood why Daniel wanted to give her his all. I couldn't be mad anymore, I understood. I would probably do the same. Chantel's sweet song came to an end and the crowd softly clapped for her. She stepped off the stage and joined me at my table.

"Cranberry Screwdriver." She held up her finger and called out to the waitress. It was obvious that she was a regular. She probably sang here often.

"Cognac?" She asked looking down at my glass.

"Mhmm." I nodded.

"I usually go for clear. It relaxes me. Makes me feel good." Chantel informed me. We were complete opposites! That's why Daniel dropped me.

"You did so well tonight. Your best performance yet, I think." The waitress said as she dropped Chantel's drink off at the table. Chantel gave her a nod as she strutted to a near table. Chantel took a sip of her drink.

"So, you sing here often?" I asked sparking up a conversation.

"Every Saturday. What do you like to do for fun?" She asked trying to keep the conversation going.

"I like to make new friends." I smiled saying the first thing that popped into my head.

"Good, because I needed a friend." Chantel grinned back taking another sip of her drink.

"How old were you when you started singing?" I asked wanting to know more about her. There was something about her that was mysterious. Something that begged you to know more about her.

"I've been singing since I was a little girl. My grandmother used to love me to sing to her. She died when I was 12 and I never stopped singing. Singing makes me feel close to her." Chantel glanced up at the stage and then back at me.

"Wow. My grandmother also died when I was a girl. She told me to stop singing. She used to say that I had a voice only a mother could love." We laughed as I lightened the mood.

"You're married?" Chantel grabbed my hand.

"Separated." I put my hand between my legs, embarrassed.

"Love is always complicated. It's a silly thing isn't it." Chantel looked for my perspective.

"Yeah. My husband couldn't stop cheating on me. I was forced to make my exit." I wasn't lying. It was sort of a half-truth.

"What an asshole. My love life is also complicated. Sometimes it's on and sometimes it's off. I learned not to stress it and just go with the flow. I'm in no rush to get anywhere and I'm not entertaining anyone else. It just is what it is with Daniel, that my boyfriend's name. He's been talking about marriage lately though." I choked on my drink as the word "marriage" slipped out of her mouth.

"Are you ok?" Chantel asked me concerned.

"Yeah. It just went down the wrong hole." I patted my chest to stop myself from choking. Chantel pulled something out of her purse and lit it. It was a blunt. I loved how carefree she was. Other people were smoking in the club as well. She took a few pulls and offered me some. I stared at it for a moment.

"Don't be scared friend, here." I took the blunt out of her hand and smoked it. I passed it back to her.

"If you wanted people to know one thing about you, what would it be?" Chantel asked me. She was just as interested in me as I was in her.

"That I'm calculated." I said without thinking.

"I've never heard any describe themselves that way. I like that. Calculated." Chantel nodded blowing out smoke and passing the blunt back to me.

"What about you?" I wondered if she would tell me something juicy.

"I don't take life so seriously. Look around. You can see that people come here to get rid of the day's troubles. Everyone is stressed out and overworked. I don't do anything I don't want to do or anything that isn't meaningful to me." She didn't do anything she didn't want to do. Daniel always said the same thing. I wondered if she got that from him or if he got it from her.

After a few hours, we exchanged a few more deep thoughts and enjoyed the jazz band. It was a really nice and laid-back club. Chantel offered to walk me to my car. I could tell the alcohol kicked in and she was getting sleepy.

When we got to my car we exchanged numbers and planned to hang out again. I opened my car door and got in. Chantel reached in my car to give me a hug and then she gave me a peck on my lips. What the fuck just happened? It took me by surprise, but I guess this is her carefree and maybe drunk self.

"Do you need a ride home or something?" I offered, worried about how she would get home safely.

"Oh, no. My boyfriend is right around the corner." She answered grinning. Oh Shit! I had to get out of there fast. I could not let Daniel see me with Chantel. He would flip.

"Okay well, I'd better get going. See you next time!" I hurriedly backed out. I wanted her to look forward to seeing me again. This was a budding friendship and I knew exactly where I wanted to take it. I had made my plan in the jazz club. I read somewhere once that your best ideas come when you're most relaxed. Your best ideas come when you're in the shower, laying down, or… in a jazz club after drinking cognac. Yeah, I knew exactly what had to be done.

When I got home, I walked in to find Mark sleeping on the couch. My stomach instantly turned. Disgust. Every fiber of my being was filled with disgust when I saw him. He was absolutely revolting. But in order for my plan to work, I had to suck it up and make amends. I pushed down the bit of vomit that crept up my throat. I gathered myself swallowing my pride. 3…2…1… and here we go.

My hand softly caressed his arm waking him up gently. He turned over and sluggishly opened his eyes.

"Come to bed Mark… Honey." The word "honey" tasted like the vomit I had just forced down. I had to change my mindset. Almost like an actress in a movie. I had a role to play and I was going to play it well.

"Are you sure?" He instantly sat up. I could see the hope in his eyes. The longing for my affection. It was like he was stranded in the desert and needed my affection as bad as he needed water. It was abundantly clear that I had been neglecting my husband. Husband. I use that term loosely. He was almost the furthest thing you could get from a husband. The truth was that he was trying but it was too little too late. Too much, actually. It was too much. I felt smothered now. But with my new plan in place, this was something I had to learn to embrace. And quickly too.

"Yes. You're right. We can't continue on like this. I want a fresh start." I grabbed his hand and stared deeply into his eyes. I needed to be convincing. I didn't want to lay it on too thick. That would alarm him. Mark nodded and followed me up the stairs into the bedroom. He slipped into our sheets while I got into the shower.

By Monday, I woke up prepared to take on my new role. I wasn't just Cynthia anymore. I was Cynthia *and* Xenia. Both personas had to be convincing. I kissed Mark on his cheek.

"Good morning, baby." I jumped out of bed and went down to make breakfast. Eggs, turkey bacon, and breakfast potatoes. That was Marks favorite breakfast. I wanted to show him that I was changing. I put on the coffee pot and started cooking. Soon after, Mark made his way into the kitchen.

"I haven't smelled this smell in a while." He sat down at the kitchen table. I smiled at him. Pouring his coffee reminded me of the cognac I had last night. I began to think of Chantel. Chantel as a person is just… captivating. It's like love radiates off of her. I didn't plan on reaching out to her. I wanted her to reach out to me.

"OW!" Fuck! I overfilled the coffee cup and spilled some on my hand. I must have gotten lost in my thoughts. I had to put Chantel on the back burner. I was just curious as to why and what it is about her that would make Daniel want to leave what we have for her. I needed to stop being obsessive over people. It was a problem I've had for a while now. I just get so caught up in other people's lives and finding out what motivates them. Why do they do the things they do and think the way they think? It was all so intriguing to me.

Between you and I, I'd probably be admitted if I let a psychologist know how I really think. But if you think about it, most therapists, psychologists, and psychiatrists are probably like me. Calculated and a little sinister. When I was in college, we learned about a therapist who implanted false memories into one of her patients. The therapist made her believe her father molested her, but it never happened. The father ended up losing everything and fought hard to prove his innocence. He sued the therapist and won. She obviously lost her license after that. It happens quite often. More than you'd think. If you think it could never and would never happen to you, you have completely underestimated the power of your thoughts and emotions in someone else's hands. You have underestimated the power of therapy.

"Are you okay?" Mark asked concerned.

"I'm fine." I replied. After making his plate, I sat it down in front of him and gave him a peck on the lips before getting ready and rushing off to work.

Chapter 4

"Anna." I greeted Anna briefly on the way to my office. I sat at my desk where she had my coffee waiting for me. I checked a few emails and responded to them. Everything in the office was running smoothly. All of the therapy and spa sessions. Work barely needed me. However, if I didn't show up I'm sure people would start slacking.

"Ma'am, you have a delivery." Anna paged my phone.

"Come in." I responded. I was calm. After I figured out my plan I was suddenly thinking clearly. Maybe I just needed to be preoccupied. Anna walked in with an enormous bouquet of roses. They were beautiful.

Red and white roses hung over the vase sides. I'm sure they're from Daniel.

Anna set the vase on my desk and walked out. I grabbed the card attached to them.

Starting over is nice. Meet me at Le Savoureux at 7 tonight. Thank you for another chance. I love you.

The bouquet was from Mark. I guess this was something. I still longed for Daniel, but I had to put those feelings to the side. If I wanted my plan to work, I needed to get rid of all emotions for everyone involved. I couldn't mess this up.

My cell phone buzzed. It was Nia checking to see if I felt better. I responded telling her I was fine. I began to wonder about how my date with Mark would go. I tried to think positively and focus on the end goal.

After work I went home, showered, and slipped into my silk red midi dress. I put on my red lipstick and put my hair in a back bun. Mark loved red on me. I wanted to make him happy.

On the drive to the restaurant, I was imagining what we would talk about. How do you reignite the spark in a dying relationship? After arriving I walked in looking for Mark sitting at a table. The restaurant was dimly lit and quiet. Whispers flew through the air. I caught Mark's eye as he held his arm up to let me know where he was. Mark stood up to pull out my chair as I walked over to our table. He took his seat after I sat down. There was already a glass of white wine waiting for me. I couldn't stand red wine. I took a sip out of the wine glass waiting for Mark to speak first.

"You look beautiful." Mark said right before taking a sip out of his glass. That was him starting the conversation and seeing where I would take it. But I didn't. I stayed quiet staring into his eyes.

"Listen. I'm so glad you came. This time I promise it's going to be different. I want to make you happy. I want you to be able to receive my affection." Mark looked nervous. I had to ease his worries.

"I want the same things, Mark. I'm tired of fighting. I'm tired of the tension. I just want you, baby. I want us. The old us." I slightly brushed my foot against his leg. The waiter came over and set our plates on the table.

"You ordered already?" I asked, almost impressed.

"I still know you like the back of my hand." Mark grinned. Only, he didn't really know me. Nobody did. I couldn't let them. He ordered the both of us the lamb chops with risotto. It was my favorite dish from this restaurant. Even though the serving sizes were a bit on the light side.

I spent the meal buttering him up and stroking his ego. I was trying to get him in the mood. After we finished our meals, we drove our separate cars home. I got home before he did. I went to our bedroom and changed into my lingerie. When Mark came in, he slowly looked me up and down. He was tempted but maintained his self-control.

"I uh… You look amazing. But I- I-" Mark stuttered. I tilted my head giving him a frown.

"I want to date you again. I don't want to rush things. I want to show you how much I appreciate you." Mark continued. I was secretly relieved. I honestly did not want to have sex with him.

"Okay. Yeah, I agree. I think that's a great idea." I nodded. We both climbed underneath the blankets. I let him hold me throughout the night.

In the morning I repeated the day before. Making coffee and Mark's favorite breakfast. I was beginning to be fine with settling into my new routine. I was satisfied. Or so I tried convincing myself. I knew myself. I knew I wouldn't be able to keep this up for long. I had to get this over with.

Mark waltzed into the kitchen giving me a kiss on the cheek before settling down at the kitchen table. He was glowing. I could see joy fall over his face. I watched him knowing that I was about to destroy him, and he had no idea.

"Honey, I want to make dinner with you tonight." I said sitting his breakfast in front of him.

"What time do you want me here, baby?" Mark took a bite of his eggs.

"I was thinking 6 O'clock. See you later. Got to run." I took a sip of his orange juice and rushed to work. On the drive to work, I decided to play hooky. I didn't really feel like going in today. I also didn't really know where I would go. I just needed to relax. I needed peace of mind. A spa! That's where I would go. I headed to the absolute best spa. It was downtown.

I went inside and asked for an hour deep tissue massage with hot rocks. They showed me to my room where I undressed and laid on the massage table. The lady came in and started on my neck and shoulders. I preferred being massaged by a woman. Men were usually too gentle with me. My plan slowly crept into my mind, but I pushed it away. I wanted my mind to be completely clear.

I enjoyed every moment of the massage. The lavender aroma kissed my nose. The music was soft and slowly put me to sleep.

After my hour was up the lady softly woke me up. I got dressed after she left the room. I checked my phone and saw I had a few text messages. One was from Chantel. I immediately opened her message.

Yoga in the park tomorrow night. 7 p.m.

I knew she would reach out. I truly hated yoga, but I did need to see Chantel again. She needed to trust me. Trust. Something I wasn't deserving of. Nobody knew it though. I can imagine you too probably have people in your life you think you can trust but can't. Happens to all of us. That makes me think about my own life. Who in my life shouldn't I trust? I think the better question would be, who could I trust? Because I didn't trust anyone. Especially because I, myself was untrustworthy.

I replied "Absolutely." And went on about my day. The rest of my day was uneventful. I decided to go shopping at a few stores. My plan played with my mind all day. I couldn't help but think of how brilliant I am. I ended up losing track of time and rushed home.

Mark had been waiting for me. He had already set the table and had been sipping on a glass of wine.

"Hey, honey! Hope I didn't keep you waiting too long." I grabbed my apron and tied it around me. Mark came into the kitchen with his glass of wine.

"Can you chop up the salad?" I asked him. I never really let him cook because he didn't know how to. He also didn't know how to take direction well. So, I left him to prepare the veggies and the salad. Mark grabbed a knife and cutting board. He began chopping up all the vegetables. I prepared the chicken. I seasoned it and sauteed it on the stove.

"How was your day honey?" Mark asked softly as if he were walking on eggshells. He probably was. He should because I wasn't the forgiving type. Not anymore.

"It was fine. Nothing too exciting. I got a massage and went to a few stores. How was your day?" I asked in return trying to be polite. I really didn't care but I pretended to. Mark probably didn't care about my day either, he was just making conversation. I thought that we would talk about the weather next. That was usually what people brought up when there was nothing else to talk about. And Mark and I had nothing else to talk about.

"It was fine. Just work and more work. My day wasn't that exciting either" Mark answered as he tossed the salad together and put some on our plates.

I finished making our plates and we ate quietly for a moment.

"I was thinking that maybe we could do something together tomorrow night." Mark looked intently at me.

"Sorry, I have plans tomorrow night." I said taking a bite of my food. I could tell Mark wanted to spend more time with me in an attempt to restore our marriage and rekindle the flame. The flame that had burned out so long ago. Mark was hopeful. Only I knew that it was too late.

"Plans?" Mark asked.

"Yes. I went to a Yoga In the Park event last week and I met a friend there. She asked me to go again tomorrow."

"Maybe some other time this week?" Mark asked still looking hopeful.

"Sure." I took a sip of my wine knowing I had other plans. The rest of the meal was silent. I thought Mark would have brought up the weather by now, but he didn't bother to.

We had finished eating and Mark grabbed both of our plates. He turned the water on and was going to wash the dishes before I stopped him.

"Don't worry about it. I'll wash the dishes." I stood up walking toward the sink.

"Are you sure?" Mark asked me confused. He knew I hated doing the dishes. But I assured him I could do them.

"I got it, honey. Just go shower and relax." I took the sponge out of his hand forcing him out of the kitchen. Before getting started, I made sure Mark was fully upstairs. I slipped on my rubber dishwashing gloves and carefully grabbed the knife Mark had used to cut up the vegetables. I rinsed the blade off to get rid of any vegetable pieces left on the knife. Then, I quickly slid it into a plastic freezer bag, making sure to place it in my work bag carefully. My mind wandered as I finished washing the dishes and putting the leftovers away. Too easy. Step 1 of my plan was complete. I knew I would sleep very well tonight. My mind was now at ease as I made my way into the shower. Mark had already fallen asleep. He used to wait for me, but things were different now. I accepted they would never be the same.

Chapter 5

        Yoga in the park had come, and I was excited to be here. This time I was prepared. I brought a big bottle of cold water and had stretched at home before coming. I scanned the park like I did the first time I came. I was looking for Chantel once again. It was almost like déjà vu. Chantel caught my eye and waved me over. I walked over to her and laid out my yoga mat. She hugged me. Chantel was excited to see me. Maybe she was just as intrigued by me as I was by her.

We did all the yoga poses; this time, it was a little easier for me. I wasn't out of breath, but I certainly broke a sweat. I could see Chantel glancing over at me in between poses to see how I was doing. I too, was sneaking a few glances at her to see how she was doing the poses. Chantel did them so effortlessly. She had probably been doing yoga for years. I enjoyed it, though. I planned on coming back every week, maybe twice per week. We watched the sunset as we did the poses. I could feel the warm sun on my face, and the cool breeze caress my skin. It was so calming. I would even say it was better than the massage I had just gotten yesterday.

Before I knew it, we were done. Everyone began rolling up their yoga mats, so I did the same.

"Stay with me." Chantel put her hand on my mat, stopping me from rolling it up.

"What?" I asked. I was confused for a moment.

"Sit with me for a while in the park. We can finish watching the sunset and just relax." Chantel smiled. I liked the whole vibe—relaxing, sunset, breeze. I couldn't turn it down. And besides, I was in no rush to go home. Home. A place I felt like I no longer had anyway. What is a home anyway?

"I'd like that." I nodded, sitting back down on my mat. I couldn't tell what kind of vibe Chantel was giving off. I didn't know if she was feeling me or if she just needed a friend. However, this was not part of the plan. I was not supposed to be friends with Chantel. I was just curious about the girl. I wanted to know what Daniel saw in her. I wanted to know how she carried herself. That was it, and now we were becoming friends. This could get messy, and I didn't want that. What if Daniel found out we were friends, or even worse? What if Chantel found out about what Daniel and I had going on? I began to feel guilty. I didn't know what to do or if I should continue hanging out with her. I also didn't want to let Yoga in The Park go because I started to like it.

Chantel went into her fanny pack and pulled out a lighter and a blunt. She put it to her lips and lit it. She then offered me some. I didn't know if I should take it or not. The ambiance was just so… indescribable. It was relaxing and intense all at the same time. Ah, what the hell? I decided to smoke it. I inhaled deeply and closed my eyes. I slowly breathed out and handed it back to her. I haven't felt like this in a long time.

"I like you. I don't have many friends, so this is nice." Chantel began to talk to me. I opened my eyes and suddenly, I noticed something. How long had it been there? All this time, I hadn't noticed it.

"Is that a ring?" I grabbed her left hand, my eyes widened.

"Yeah. My fiancé just proposed yesterday." Chantel snatched her hand back and glared down at her hand. "I don't know if I want to do it, though. You never know if you're making the right decision. Especially with someone you've been through hell and back with. I accepted the engagement and the ring. I don't know if I accept the marriage, though." Chantel explained. She almost looked embarrassed. I could tell she didn't want to make eye contact with me.

"I know what you mean. I just try to choose happiness and peace. I don't waste my time if something doesn't bring me those things. I learned the hard way." I took the blunt out of her hand, taking a hit.

"I've always tried to be that way, which is why I'm here. I've always felt connected to the Earth, the sun, the wind, and the water. The beach is my favorite place in the world to be. Your whole world could be falling apart, but when you go to the beach… It's like everything is suddenly okay in the world. It just washes away your worries." I could relate to everything that Chantel said. She was right.

"I feel that way about the rain too. I love crisp, cold, rainy days. I love watching the raindrops fall down a window." I placed my hand on Chantel's thigh. She smiled, so I left it there for a minute.

"Have you ever connected with someone on a deeper level right away? You don't know why but it's their energy that pulls you in." Chantel asked me. I didn't know if she was talking about Daniel or me. Quite frankly, to answer her question, I didn't know if I was replying about her or Daniel. I didn't know how to answer her question. I felt myself getting high. I hit me swiftly and suddenly. I sat there for a moment, closing my eyes. I embraced the breeze on my face. It was getting stronger as the sun went down.

"Ye-" Before I could answer, Chantel's lips were on my lips. Her lips were full and soft. She kissed me delicately. Her kiss was like silk sliding over my mouth. She was feeling me. Maybe a little more than I was feeling her. Maybe, exactly how I was feeling her. I didn't know how I was feeling. Confused, you could say.

My stomach quivered. Butterflies were flying all around my stomach. I couldn't stop kissing her. There was lust and passion and fire. I haven't felt like this in a long time. Not even Daniel made me feel this way. Maybe she made Daniel feel like this, though. That's why he wanted to marry her. Shit, even I wanted to marry her. Chantel grabbed my face and pulled me in closer. At this point, she could take me right here. I wanted her to.

No. This was not part of the plan. I didn't want it to get any more complicated and scandalous than it already was. I pulled back, covering my mouth with my hand. Chantel put her head down, biting her lip. She had a shy smile on her face. I knew it was time to go.

"I want to take you somewhere." I whispered, knowing I had to leave, but I just couldn't. Chantel looked at me, her smile grew wider. This was a bad idea, but I was falling deep. I couldn't stop myself, and I didn't want to. I just wanted to live in the moment.

We packed up our mats and ran to my car like cackling giddy schoolgirls. I couldn't help but admire her beauty when we got in the car. I was amazed at how the sun radiated off her skin and made her glow. I got lost staring at her. I leaned over, kissing her again. I could admire her all day and night. This time Chantel pulled back, waiting for me to drive.

I started the car and pulled off hurriedly. Our destination was twenty minutes away. I wanted to get there before the sun completely went down.

We made it just in time. It was my favorite beach. It was usually empty and quiet. The best sunsets happened here. One side of the beach had giant boulders that the waves crashed into. It made a roaring yet beautiful sound. The ocean was a gentle ferocious beast, like me.

"Come on!" I exclaimed. We rushed out of the car. Chantel took me by the hand as we ran towards the water. We watched the sun finally go completely down. We soaked our feet in the salty water. We kicked it at each other, ran from the waves, and buried our toes in the sand. We thoroughly enjoyed the beach together. When we settled down, she rested her head on my shoulder.

"I don't want this to end. You have a fiancé and a whole situation going on." I rested my hand on her inner thigh.

"Do you ever just enjoy the moment? It's as if your mind is always running a thousand miles every minute." Chantel answered me without answering me. I knew what she meant, and she was right. I still needed an answer. What was this and what was going to happen to us? Did I need to readjust my plan or not? No, I had to stick to the plan. It was perfect. I had to leave all feelings to the side. Friend or foe, nothing was getting in the way. Feelings always ruin good things.

"I try not to label anything. This is why even having a fiancé is weird. I don't know what this is or where it's going, but nobody can ruin this but us. Maybe our feelings will change tomorrow or next week. Maybe not. Just go along with the flow. Like the ocean." Chantel gave me a peck on the cheek. I didn't say much after that. There was nothing to say. I wanted to hold back and embrace her at the same time. Chantel seemed like the kind of person that everyone cared about but cared about no one or anything. I was the opposite to some extent. I cared about everyone, but no one seemed to care about me. People like this always seemed to find each other. It's the biggest reason why I am the way I am. I needed to create some space between us. I could see exactly how this would end. Anyone would think I caught feelings too fast. But the truth is, emotions are hard and complicated. I've never felt like this about anyone this fast before. It was something about her. You don't come across people like her regularly. Every touch drew me in more and more. Every kiss made me want more and more.

"Let's go!" I demanded. We headed back to the car. Our pants were wet and sandy. I grabbed a towel out of my trunk. We took turns wiping down our legs. The sand wouldn't come off our pants. We eagerly took them off. We ran into the car before anyone could see us, even though it was already dark and the street was dimly lit. I turned the heater on. It was freezing. I blew inside my hands and rubbed them together before placing them in front of the heater. Chantel took my hands in hers and rubbed them. I began to warm up. I leaned in to kiss her again. Chantel started rubbing my clit. It felt so good, but everything in me told me to stop. I wanted to see where this would go. So, I let her. I took my panties off and climbed to the back seat. She followed.

She climbed on top of me as I maneuvered to lay across the seats. Chantel kissed my lips, she slowly moved down to my ear, before placing her sweet lips on my neck. She took her time with me. She was very delicate. Chantel treated me as if my body would break. I usually liked it rough, but this time was different.

One of her locs fell across my face. I left it there. Her hair smelled nice, like vanilla and chamomile. I could feel Chantel's kisses move down my body, stopping at my chest. She lifted my shirt and pulled my titty out of my bra. She took me in her mouth.

I had never had sex with a woman before. It was… different. I think I liked it a little better. I didn't have to tell her what to do, where to move, how soft or hard to kiss me. It was like she already knew my body. It was like my body belonged to her. My body was hers.

Suddenly I felt Chantel's fingers inside me. I let out a soft gasp. My moans grew louder and faster as she went in and out of me. Gentle and slow, then suddenly hard and fast, then slow again. The rhythm of her fingers changed at the right moment. Chantel took her fingers out of me and stuck them in her mouth, sucking my juices off of her. She stared deeply into my eyes as if she was gazing at my soul. Everything seemed to be happening in slow motion. I let out a small gasp; my breathing grew louder.

Chantel threw my legs in the air and put my pussy in her mouth. It felt so good. This was the best head I had gotten in a while. I could tell she had done this before. Her tongue played with my clit. I let out another moan surrendering to her touch. Fuck, this felt so good!

"Yes. Don't stop." I whispered loudly. I didn't want her to stop. I put my hand on the back of her head. Unfortunately, one of our phones started going off. Chantel sat up precipitously, climbing to the front seat. She settled in the passenger seat, rummaging through her fanny pack to find her phone.

"Hey, baby." Chantel answered her phone, turning her attention out the window. She purposely avoided eye contact with me as I made my way into the driver's seat. Tuning her out, I looked intently at the waves crashing against the rocks. Leave it to Daniel to ruin a moment. I mean, I was with his fiancé. Daniel had every right to ruin the moment. Acknowledging that, still didn't make it any easier. Horniness took over my body. I squirmed in my seat while cracking the car window. The fresh air aroused me even more. I hate to admit. Chantel placed her hand on my shoulder, startling me and bringing me back to reality.

"Can you take me back to my car? I think we lost track of time" Once again, there was a smile on her face.

The same smile that drew me in. I could tell she wasn't at all bothered by the phone call she had just received.

"Was that your boo?" I asked nosily. Chantel only nodded, refusing to go into detail. Trying not to pry any further, I ignored her for the rest of the ride. We both enjoyed the car ride and the music in the background.

After pulling up to her car, she gave me a few pecks on the lips before leaving. I didn't know how to feel.

I felt a little numb. Numb; a feeling where you are completely desensitized to all feeling, or you are tingly all over. I didn't know which numb I felt. I couldn't explain it. Even though I had these… confused feelings about Chantel, I secretly had love for Daniel. Even though I hated to admit it.

Things between Daniel and I were nothing short of passionate. A passion, a fire that I had never felt before, he was familiar. Chantel felt nice, different. My feelings for her were very unfamiliar. I didn't recognize them. That is why I was so confused. I was getting to a point where I didn't recognize myself. I felt hurt, confused, happy, and crazy. Daniel made me feel like a slow R&B song. There were so many more emotions that I couldn't put into words. I know he still thought about me. Or at least I hoped he did, like I thought about him. I would also bet he wasn't thinking about me like most people in my life.

I couldn't help it. I was too much in my head. I picked up my phone. I only stared at it. My thumb grazed over the phone screen. I bit my lip, not knowing what to do next. This was part of the plan, right? Maybe I should call before Chantel got home. I dialed his number before I could convince myself not to. I listened to the phone ring and ring, and ring some more. Finally, he answered.

"Daniel!" I exhaled. Great, now what was I supposed to say? I wasn't counting on him answering.

"Cynthia." Daniel waited for me to speak. I thought I would become flustered, but his familiarity always gave me a warm feeling.

"Listen, I know you probably don't want to speak to me right now, but just hear me out. I know your mind is made up, and there is nothing I can do or say to change that. I just… I guess what I'm trying to say is… I just need to see you one more time to… gain closure." The words poured out of my mouth before I knew what I was saying. Besides the warm feeling, there was nothing else. I had become focused on what I planned to do. It was like I was a machine. During this call, I removed myself and my feelings from the situation. I waited patiently for Daniel's response. It seemed like an hour had gone by before he responded.

"Uh… yea, sure. But I can't keep doing this with you, Cynthia. This is the last time." Daniel hesitated. I could tell he didn't want to meet up with me, but he couldn't hold back, just like I couldn't. Seeing him after this wasn't part of the plan, so I agreed and gave him an address to write down. I needed him to meet me in the back of an alley We planned to meet up tomorrow night. This was our final goodbye.

Chapter 6

That morning, Mark felt too sick to go to work. It must've been something he ate. It may have been a sleight of hand while I prepared his plate last night while he wasn't looking. I took advantage of his sickness and decided to take Mark's car instead of my own. I liked his a little more than my own. It was a bright red sports car. Something that demanded your attention. I loved driving fast on the highway with the windows down and the wind striking my face.

I headed to say my goodbyes to Daniel in the bright red sports car. It made me feel edgy, dangerous even. It gave me the confidence to finally walk away after our last and final goodbye.

I pulled into the back alleyway where I told Daniel to meet me. Needing time to ease the butterflies in my stomach and get out of my own head, I deliberately arrived early. I fixed my hair and my lipstick in my mirror, feeling the need to look presentable. But secretly, I wanted to look attractive. Not like I was trying too hard. I wanted to appear effortlessly attractive. Daniel needed to be reminded of why he wanted to start fucking me to begin with. He needed to be reminded of who he was fucking with.

A short while later, Daniel pulled into the alleyway and parked on the side of my car. I got out of my car and got into his. I could hear my deep and shallow breaths. I tried to gain control of my breathing before getting into Daniel's car.

"How have you been?" My nerves had eluded me. Finally, I gained control of my breath. That didn't stop the conversation from being awkward.

"I've been good. Cynthia, I want you to know…" Daniel paused briefly. I used his pause as an opportunity to look him over. To take every piece of him in one last time. His muscles, his eyes, his lips; I embraced it all. I appreciated him in ways I knew Chantel didn't. Because of the carefree spirit she possessed, I knew it was impossible for her to appreciate him the way I did. Chantel cherished nature the way I loved and cherished Daniel. She could never have the same regard for human life the way she loved, valued, and cared for Mother Earth. For that, I was envious.

"I still have feelings for you." Daniel finished his sentence. I couldn't let *feelings* get in the way of anything. I didn't want him to change my mind. The sincerity in his eyes drew me in. I looked down at my sweaty palms, wiping them on my pants. My knees started to tremble as my eyes welled up with tears. My chest felt heavy, it became more difficult to breathe with every breath I took. With perspiring hands, I reached in the back of my pants and wrapped my clammy fingers around the handle, making sure to get a good grip on it. I took in a deep breath and pursed my lips, not knowing what would come next but preparing for the worst. All I knew was that I had a plan to stick to. Could I really pull it off?

Before he could say anything else, I cautiously slithered it out of the back of my pants and gouged it into his abdomen. Once, twice, three times being careful not to get any blood on my clothes. Daniel looked at me in disbelief as he grabbed hold of the bloody blade. Disbelief was an understatement. I would remember that look forever. It was burned into my memory. We held on to separate ends of the knife together as I watched the life drain from his sorrowful eyes. I could tell he regretted meeting up with me.

I couldn't let him finish pouring his heart out to me. That would ruin everything. The damage was done when he completely humiliated me by breaking my heart and calling our affair quits, even if Chantel was the reason. This had to be the last and final goodbye.

"I'm sorry, Daniel. I had to. Goodbye." That was all I could think to say. I couldn't bear giving him an explanation as he struggled to catch every breath in efforts to fight for his life. A fight he was losing. I closed my eyes as the tears finally fell from them. I wanted to tell him I loved him. I wanted to tell him the feeling was mutual, that I still had feelings for him too. But I couldn't. I knew if either of us continued, I wouldn't be able to go on with my plan. With Chantel in the picture, I couldn't go back to the drawing board and think of a whole new plan. I just wanted to lie with him. I wanted him to take his last breath with me. I was incapable of staying with him until then. I couldn't bear it. I ran back into my car. I took off my blood-soaked gloves and placed them in a plastic bag, making sure not to get a single drop on myself. I drove off quickly, but not quickly enough to draw any attention to myself.

Daniel may have very well been the love of my life. But he didn't love me the way I loved him, and that was his fatal mistake. This is why feelings never mattered to me. I always felt more intensely for others than they felt for me. Maybe that was a good thing. Because in the end, it made me who I am today.

After pulling into our garage, I stuffed the bloody gloves under the driver's seat of the sporty red car. Do you understand my plan now? Two birds, one stone. Surely, you understand. I was tired of getting hurt. I wouldn't allow it anymore. We've all felt this way before. Or maybe I was the only one who was this… calculated.

I scurried inside the dark house like a sneaky mouse. I stumbled over the steps carefully to ensure I wouldn't fall. Making sure not to wake Mark, I snuck into the shower. Honestly, I didn't feel like talking to him or filling him in about my day. I didn't care if he got enough rest or not.

The scolding water washed away all my worries. It was as if nothing had happened at all. And that's precisely how I would act, like nothing happened. There were no feelings of guilt, remorse, pain, or anything. I felt nothing. I let the scorching hot water hit my face and drip down my body washing my troubling day away. Everything was all right in the world now, at least it would be.

Obviously, I knew that I would lose Mark. The unfortunate truth was that I had already lost him many times over the course of our marriage. No matter how much I yearned for him, no matter how much I cried for him, I never got him back. The man I loved as my husband and best friend was gone. Many years ago, I was forced to mourn him, our marriage, and everything we built together. I was left with the remnants of the man I once loved; the remnants of the marriage I was once happy in. The man I lived with now was an unfamiliar stranger. Therefore, it didn't bother me to get rid of him.

However, I would mourn Daniel. I never had to before, so I knew it would be hard. Daniel never did anything wrong to me during the course of our involvement. We got along great, actually. The passion I had for him convinced me that he felt the same about me, but it's clear that I was wrong once again.

I was tired of the same story from different men. I just wanted someone to care about me the way I cared about them; to prioritize me. Unfortunately, I knew it would never happen. Not anytime soon, anyway.

I had to stay focused on what was to come next. That would be an investigation, arrest, Chantel getting her heart broken, etc. Initially, I hadn't planned on being present for Chantel's heartbreak, but I knew that now I would have to comfort her. I wasn't great at the whole comforting thing. It was all a little too melodramatic for me. Wishful thinking had me hoping that my and Chantel's situation would be enough to distract from her grief, but I knew that wouldn't be the case.

I rinsed all the suds off my body and rushed to get out of the shower. I needed to prepare for tomorrow's troubles.

Again, I woke up, made breakfast, showered, and headed into the office. I wondered what would happen next. Would Daniel's death be on the news? Would the police visit me at my office? Would Chantel call me crying? Who knew? To be honest, it wasn't my problem anymore. It was out of my hands, and everything would take care of itself.

At work that morning, I didn't have much to do. I sipped on my coffee while checking my emails. I didn't have anything to do. Eventually, I wound up just sitting around twiddling my thumbs when my door suddenly flew open. Nia came waltzing into my office. She was clearly in a good mood. Nia plopped down in one of my chairs.

"Guess what I did last night!" Nia ran her tongue across the front of her teeth with a sinister smile. She couldn't have done anything half as bad as me.

"I'm sure you're going to tell me." I tapped my pen on the desk, waiting to hear her crazy story.

"I had my first one-night stand!" Nia squealed. I desperately wanted to scream out how I killed Daniel last night. But obviously, I couldn't do that.

"Oooo… Tell me more." I leaned in closer to her, intrigued by the beginning of her story.

"Girl, I decided to go to the bar last night and met this *fine* man. I just had to take him home. Well, he took me home and fucked the shit out of me. This man had my legs all up in the air; I was in all kinds of positions." Nia and I laughed hysterically, giving each other high fives.

"I remember those days. Whew, we need to go out together, and see what trouble I can get into." I smiled, reminiscing.

"You don't need to get into any more trouble." Nia teased. She had no idea just how right she was.

"You got that right." I said right before there was a knock on my door again. Two men in suits walked in. They were both tall, dark, and handsome. They introduced themselves as Detective Williams and Detective Jones. Nia turned to me. Her eyes grew wide.

"Detectives, can I help you with something?" I calmly asked. In my mind, nothing happened.

"Just a couple of questions regarding a Mr. Daniel Smith." Detective Jones announced. Nia's eyes grew even wider as she dropped her jaw.

"Sure. What is it?" I asked innocently, standing up out of my chair.

"You had a call with Mr. Smith a couple of days ago. What was it regarding?" Detective Jones pulled out a pen and notepad, preparing to take notes.

"Daniel and I were having an affair. My husband found out about it. I was unsure about how he would react or what would happen, so I called Daniel to let him know. Just in case my husband wanted to give him a call or something. Why?" Nia gasped. She covered her mouth as I spoke.

"Is that why you went MIA on me?" Nia shouted. I hadn't planned on this, but it was the perfect story. I nodded at Nia. The detective scribbled swiftly on his notepad.

"Did your husband threaten him or you at all, in any kind of way?" asked Detective Williams. I could see the concern as the "ah ha" moment washed over his grim-looking face.

"No, sir. Mark is harmless." I wanted to sound like every other wife who "protects" her husband. I knew they were already looking at him as a suspect, so I didn't need to put in anymore work.

"Where can we find Mark now?" Detective Williams inquired. I grabbed a sticky note and jotted down the address to Mark's office. Detective Jones pointed at the sticky note and told me to write down Mark's last name as well, so I did.

"Should I be concerned? Is everything okay?" I asked while handing him the sticky note.

"I'm sorry to inform you that Mr. Smith was found stabbed to death in an alleyway, ma'am. That is the only information we can give at this time." Detective Jones closed his notebook.

"What? Are you sure?" I exclaimed in mock disbelief.

"Oh my God, Cynthia!" Nia jumped out of her chair to console me. Tears fell down my face. The shock and the disbelief were fake, but the tears were real. I was hurt over what had to be done. The detectives gave their condolences and headed out. Nia held me while I wept. I could tell she wanted to tell me, "I told you so," but I knew she wouldn't.

"Cynthia, I'm so sorry. You need to stay at my place for a couple of nights. I won't let you go back home." Nia wiped my tears and started grabbing my belongings. She wouldn't take no for an answer. Therefore, I wasn't going to fight her on it. Most likely, no arrests were going to be made for a couple of days, so I didn't know how long I would be at Nia's.

That evening after work, I arrived at Nia's. She gave me some extra clothes so that I could take a shower and get comfortable. After my shower, she had a glass of wine waiting on me on the living room coffee table. Nia was an amazing friend. She's the one person in my life that always looked out for me and had my back. Honestly, I couldn't ask for a better friend. Even though Nia was the most trustworthy person that I had, I couldn't trust her with the truth. If I couldn't trust her with this, I couldn't trust anyone. I sat down next to her and picked up my glass of wine.

"Friend, are you okay." Nia put her shoulder around me. I rested my head on her.

"No. This is all my fault." A tear escaped from the side of my eye. At least I was somewhat telling the truth.

"If I hadn't had an affair, Daniel would be alive and… And... I don't know what's going to happen to Mark."

"Cynthia, he's going to jail. Prison! You can't blame yourself, love. Nobody could've known that this was going to happen. I mean, to look at things on a positive note, we don't actually know that Mark did anything. Come on Cynthia, you know Mark's not like that. *We* know he's not like that." Nia shook her head and squeezed me tighter.

"Then why did you tell me to stay here?" I uttered.

"Nobody said to be stupid. Better safe than sorry." Nia wiped my tears and kissed my head. Isn't it ironic that she was trying to protect me from a murderer, and the murderer was sitting right next to her the whole time?

I checked my phone repeatedly. From the corner of my eye, I could see Nia watching me. She thought I was checking my phone for Mark, but I was checking it for Chantel.

A news report came on the tv about Daniel's death. Nia changed the channel. She pretended like the news of Daniel hadn't just come on as she flipped through channels. Out of nowhere, my phone went off. It was Mark. Nia jumped and grabbed her chest. We exchanged nervous looks.

"Mark, baby?" I said calmly.

"Hi, honey. I was just wondering what time you would be home?" It didn't seem like the police talked to him unless he was playing it cool.

"I won't be coming home tonight. I… I… Uhm, just slammed at work, you know, and I thought I'd spend the night at Nia's since it's closer to work. I didn't want to drive tired." As the words slowly slithered out of my mouth, Nia was franticly waving her hands in the air. I widened my eyes at her, not knowing why she was doing that or what she was trying to say. I rushed off the phone with Mark to see what Nia was trying to tell me.

"Bitch! What is wrong with you?" Nia was clearly upset.

"What?" I was a little perplexed.

"What in the fuck would possess you to tell that man that you're at my house?" Nia poured herself another glass of wine, guzzling it down, waiting for my answer.

"I'm sorry. I wasn't thinking, but from our conversation, it doesn't seem like the cops even spoke to him" I tried calming her down. I wasn't petrified because I was the murderer. Maybe Nia should be because the murderer was closer than she thought.

"Yeah, he was trying to lure you home so you could be next!" Nia sat her wine down.

"You're the one who said he probably didn't do it." I reminded her. She didn't know just how true that statement was. Nia rubbed her temples. I watched as the thoughts ran rampant through her head; she was trying to think of a way to calm the both of us down.

"You're right. I'm sorry. I'm sorry." Nia apologized to me. I almost felt bad for putting her in this position, for making her worry, and for making her think that both of our lives may potentially be in danger.

"I think we should go to bed. Goodnight, Nia." Making her feel bad further pushed the narrative I created. I didn't enjoy seeing her like this. However, I had to protect myself. I would do whatever it took to do that. I headed to the guest room and shut the door behind me.

As soon as my head hit the pillow, I drifted off to sleep. The soft, shaggy duvet engulfed me. To be quite honest, I thought it would be difficult to fall asleep that night. It wasn't. I slept peacefully that night.

Chapter 7

I woke up with my phone vibrating. I had a text message from Chantel. My eyes widened. I rushed to open the message.

> I need to talk to you. Can you meet me for coffee this morning at Five Beans?

Chantel probably found out about Daniel now. Nia busted into the room before I could gather my thoughts.

"They arrested Mark!" She grabbed the tv remote and turned on the news immediately. We watched as the newscaster explained that the police had obtained an emergency search warrant for our home and Mark's cars. They came in the middle of the night to surprise him. The news explained how Mark's car was seen on cameras driving toward the alleyway and that he had a motive. After searching his vehicle, the officers found the bloody knife and the glove in the car. After taking him into custody, they were able to confirm that the fingerprints on the knife were in fact, his.

That's it. My plan worked perfectly. I would say I couldn't believe it, but I could. My steps were carefully planned, and they were unfolding just as I intended. I watched Nia's jaw drop. It was like I was watching her in slow motion. She then turned towards me shaking her head with tears in her eyes.

"I'm so sorry." Nia hugged me tightly. What she didn't know was that I had already grieved. I was over it. I squeezed my eyes tightly, trying to force out a tear or two.

"I have to go." I gently pushed Nia off me and threw on some comfortable clothes. She briefly watched me get dressed. She didn't know what to do.

"Ok, I understand. I'm sorry, Cynthia." Nia sniffled and wiped her tears away. Nia stopped at the door turning towards me.

"At some point, you have to deal with this Cynthia. Not now, but you will." Nia finally left, closing the door behind her.

I brushed my teeth and texted Chantel back:

Normally I would've said "Of course" or "Definitely" but I didn't want to sound too eager. On the drive over, I wondered if Chantel had seen the news. I wondered if she knew Mark was my husband. I had intentionally never told her his name. Hell, she didn't even know my name. I mean, I never planned on dragging Chantel along, but I couldn't get rid of her now. I didn't want to.

I walked into the coffee shop. It was a local coffee shop. Go figure. Chantel was the type of person to support local and small businesses. The aroma of rich and fresh ground coffee beans engulfed me. I loved the smell of fresh coffee, especially on a cold, gloomy morning like today.

Chantel was nowhere to be found in the small coffee shop. I ordered a small black coffee before sitting at a table next to the window. It was the perfect seat to watch the raindrops hit the window if it just so happened to rain. I looked up at the clouds and decided it probably wasn't going to rain though.

I began to people-watch. People are interesting. Mostly oblivious to what's going on around them. Self-absorbed. Self-absorbed, only caring about themselves, selfish. Selfish, self-absorbed people create a dangerous and chaotic society. I am the product of those types of people. People like that create people like me; they didn't even realize it. They would probably never realize it. That's the scary thing about selfish people: people like me.

Chantel plopped down in the seat in front of me, suspending my thoughts. I gave her a shy smile and took a sip of my hot coffee. Chantel had some sort of tea. She didn't smile back, maintaining a sad and somber look. I knew what that meant.

"How is it going? Did you need something?" I delivered her a script I had thought about two seconds ago, pretending to be oblivious to her pain. Chantel slowly nodded before looking up at me so she could speak.

"My friend Daniel, well, my ex. I watched the news this morning. He's the guy that was stabbed in the alleyway." Chantel was choked up and failing to fight back her tears. Did she mean "friend" or "ex"? They were engaged, weren't they?

"I'm sorry, I just didn't know who to call." Chantel stared out the window, collecting herself so she could continue.

"No, it's fine. I'm so sorry, Chantel. Tell me about Daniel." I reached out and grabbed her hand to help calm her down. I needed to get all the details out because now I was confused about what the hell was going on and what I had done. On a positive note, at least I wasn't involved with Daniel's fiancé, right? Unless they had just broken things off, had they?

"Ok, well…" Chantel took a deep breath before starting again.

"Daniel and I were together for like five years. He broke things off last year. Said he wanted to explore his sexuality. He was gay. Six months later, he married a man. We still were very close friends. I understood what he was going through. He left our pictures up on social media because he wasn't ready to come out to his family. I still hung out with him and his husband. We all became close friends. And now, he's dead. They arrested some guy this morning or last night, I don't know." Chantel began to sob loudly. I shushed her and rubbed her arm. I was putting pieces of the puzzle together. I consoled her but I was really buying time to console myself.

Daniel, gay?! Daniel was exploring his sexuality. That's why he was stringing me along. That's why he broke things off with me. He was no longer exploring; he knew what he wanted. Daniel just didn't trust me with the truth like he trusted Chantel. I can see why, honestly.

I killed Daniel for breaking my heart. Things might've ended differently if I had known he was struggling with his sexuality. I wouldn't have been able to kill him if I'd known the truth. Daniel should have told me the truth; it would have saved his life. Lies and selfish people ruin the world.

Chantel wept in her hands. Her phone suddenly rang. Chantel composed herself before answering. She wasn't on the phone long. A few "uh-huh's" and "yeps" before hanging up the phone.

"That was my fiancé. He uh… He was upset this morning because I'm so torn up about Daniel. He doesn't think I should have feelings for my ex. Even if we weren't still friends I would be torn apart about his death. We got into a big argument, and I stormed out. Daniel was a very good person. He was so fun and… and full of life."

Chantel smiled remembering him. She was thinking about the good times they had spent together.

Chantel's fiancé didn't seem like he deserved her. Not like I did. Chantel was gentle. She's special. Chantel didn't deserve someone like him. She deserved better. Chantel deserved me, the best parts of me, and I deserved her. All of her.

"He sounds like a great person. It's great that he was able to be so honest with you." I said sarcastically, but Chantel couldn't tell. I was a little jealous that Daniel could be honest with her but not with me.

"He was. Daniel was an amazing person. Listen, I uh… I have to head back to my apartment. Sage, my fiancé, locked himself out of the apartment, he needs to grab something for work. Do you want to come? It won't take long."

I agreed. We got in her car, and she sped towards her place. The drive wasn't long, five minutes, maybe. The coffee shop was close to her apartment. That's probably why she wanted to meet there.

The time had finally come for me to meet this infamous fiancé, Sage. Thoughts of Sage and his personality consumed me. I wondered what he looked like. I already knew he was an asshole that I didn't care for. I followed her into the elevator. We went up seven floors before the elevator door chimed. Chantel stepped off the elevator while I continued to follow behind her. We walked down the long, well-lit hall to her apartment.

Sage was sitting on the floor outside of her door. I didn't like the way he carried himself. I mean, he was sitting on the floor of an apartment building. How gross? Don't get me wrong, the apartment was clean and very well kept, but the thought of sitting on a public floor made my stomach turn. Sage seemed like the kind of guy Chantel would go for. He was carefree and a little dingy.

Chantel opened the door for him. Sage stormed into the apartment grabbing something and scurried right back out. He didn't acknowledge me. He acted as if I weren't even there at all. Probably because he was in a rush or maybe because he was used to Chantel bringing home strangers. Either way, it didn't bother me. It allowed me to be a fly on the wall for a split second and observe the way they interacted with one another. I didn't care to speak to him anyway.

Chantel invited me in. I made myself comfortable on her couch while she made herself comfortable on my lap. My lap held her head. I massaged her scalp, watching her come to grips with losing her friend. The pain was all over her face even though she tried to hide it. I wanted to dig deeper into her soul. I wanted to know her inside out. I wanted to know what was happening between us or even what could potentially happen. In my mind, there was no "potentially" it *was* going to happen because I was going to make it happen.

"You said Daniel struggled with his sexuality or was trying to explore it. Are you also exploring your sexuality or…?" I had to know because I needed to see where she saw us going. Was it a one-time thing or what?

"Oh, ha-ha. I see. The answer to your question is no; I am not exploring my sexuality. I know I am bi, and I'm comfortable with who I am." Chantel smiled. We both knew where this line of questioning was going and she seemed prepared for it.

"I wanted to know, are we just friends, or are we a little more? Do you want to be more?" I pried. Chantel grabbed the back of my head and pulled my face down to hers. She kissed me passionately. I began to throb. I had to have her.

"I like you Xenia, I do. But we're just friends. There is a lot going on with me. I don't want to further complicate my life right now. I mean, I barely want to be with Sage. I hope you understand." Cynthia sat up from my lap after delivering those gut-wrenching words.

It felt like a literal punch to the gut. Why was this happening again? Was it me? Am I the problem? Somebody is going to love me. That somebody was going to be Chantel. Even if she didn't know it yet, she would. I had a plan.

It didn't matter what I had to do. I would have Chantel. I wouldn't allow anyone to stop me or to get in my way, not her and not Sage.

To Be Continued…